JPL discards materials that are outdated and in poor condition. In order to make room for current, in-demand materials, underused materials are offered for public sale

Super Ben's Broken Cookie:
A Book About Sharing
by Shelley Marshall   **Illustrated by Ben Mahan**

Super Ben does not always share. Can you help Super Ben share? Let's read!

Enslow Elementary
an imprint of
Enslow Publishers, Inc.
40 Industrial Road
Box 398
Berkeley Heights, NJ 07922
USA

http://www.enslow.com

What a great day for a picnic! Yum!

Wait a minute. What does Ben have?

"May I please have some?" asks Molly.

"No. This cookie is special," Ben says.

"Why?" asks Molly.

"It's special because it's mine."

"Hi Molly! Hi Ben!"

"Look! There is Mai," says Molly.

"Check out her new bike!" says Ben.

"May I have a turn?" Ben asks.

"Sure!" says Mai.

Bonk!

"Oh, sorry," Juan says.

"Hey!" says Molly. "May we play too?"

"Sure!" says Juan.

17

Uh-oh. Something is falling out of Ben's pocket.

"What is that?" Mai asks.

Oh no! What should Ben do?

Ben thinks about Mai's bike.
He thinks about Juan's ball.

"Do you want some?"
Ben asks.

"Yes!"

Ben shares his cookie.
Sharing feels great!

23

Read More About Sharing

Books

Bardhan-Quallen, Sudipta. *Mine-o-saur*. New York: GP Putnam's Sons, 2007.

Cole, Joanna. *Sharing Is Fun*. New York: HarperCollins, 2004.

Web Site

Kids Next Door
www.hud.gov/kids/people.html

Enslow Elementary, an imprint of Enslow Publishers, Inc.

Enslow Elementary® is a registered trademark of Enslow Publishers, Inc.

Library of Congress Cataloging-in-Publication Data
Marshall, Shelley, 1968-
  Super Ben's broken cookie : a book about sharing / Shelley Marshall.
    p. cm. — (Character education with Super Ben and Molly the Great)
  ISBN 978-0-7660-3514-0
  1. Sharing in children—Juvenile literature. 2. Sharing—Juvenile literature.
3. Conduct of life—Juvenile literature. I. Title.
  BF723.S428M37 2010
  177'.7—dc22
                            2009000498

ISBN-13: 978-0-7660-3739-7 (paperback edition)

Printed in the United States of America

112009 Lake Book Manufacturing, Inc., Melrose Park, IL

10 9 8 7 6 5 4 3 2 1

To Our Readers: We have done our best to make sure all Internet Addresses in this book were active and appropriate when we went to press. However, the author and the publisher have no control and assume no liability for the material available on those Internet sites or on other Web sites they may link to. Any comments or suggestions can be sent by e-mail to comments@enslow.com or to the address on the back cover.